FOSSIL BEDS BED & BREAKFAST

Siobhan Muir

THREE LAKES BOOKS, LLC

ISBN: 9781947221321

Published by Three Lakes Books

Cover Design: Kris Norris

Second Electronic Print, February 2025

CONTENTS

Maya Sorino loves her life in Deadman, Wyoming. She has two great kids, a successful bed & breakfast, and enough room to freely roam as her dino self. Everything is perfect. Until a rich developer comes to town, trying to undermine her business and seize the town's open land. Not on her watch.

Persia Walker has been guarding the fossil rich lands since she almost became one, but she won't let a billionaire destroy sacred paleo sites for vanity. She organizes a group to take on the developer at the public meeting in hopes of preserving her territory. Then she sees Maya.

Finding another dinosaur shifter in Deadman is a dream for both Maya and Persia, but the developer has something up his sleeve. What's a better first date than going Mesozoic on a bunch of drunk vandals-for-hire? It's a match made in Prehistory!

This story was previously published in the Cretaceous Crushes LGBTQ+ Romance Charity Anthology. It has been expanded and given a new cover.

DEDICATION

Dedicated to all the "little people" who stand up against big money because it's the right thing to do. You're why we still have lovely things to enjoy.

ACKNOWLEDGMENTS

I know I say this every time, but writing a book is never really a one-person job, and writing a series is especially difficult alone. Keeping track of details from previous stories is so much easier when you have help. Not only does it take a great deal of hard work, editing, and research on the part of the author to get things correct, but without my compatriots, there'd be a lot more mistakes.

Huge thanks to Kelex for suggesting this story idea to begin with. Without the Cretaceous Crushes LGBTQIA Romance Charity Anthology, I wouldn't have had a chance to write about my favorite dinosaur in shifter form. Besides, there's room in LGBTQIA romance for dino shifters. Great thanks to Susan Sailors for over my story for big gaps and word usage. Thanks also to Aerin Varhalmi for catching all my typos and missed words! And great thanks to Kris Norris for designing the cover.

As always, great thanks to my readers for cheering me on. Y'all make my writing worth the detailed effort.

CHAPTER ONE

M aya took a deep breath as she settled on the front deck of the Fossil Beds B&B with a fresh cup of peppermint tea. The summer weather in Deadman, Wyoming was just the most perfect it had been in this century—and she knew weather. She loved when the world turned green and lush from the afternoon and evening thunderstorms, and the mornings dawned fresh with dew on all the surfaces.

Absolute perfection.

She kicked her feet up on the railing and listened to the birds chirping with their territorial songs. She still spoke their languages, a modified version of the same sounds she remembered from her teenage years when she'd migrated with her family across much of what was now northern Montana. Of course, back then, the language had been spoken by what humans named velociraptors, Compsognathus, and other small predators. Sue the Tyrannosaur had used that language, too, but she'd been a mean, crotchety old bitch, and Maya hadn't been sad to hear of her passing.

Over the millennia, the evolutionary tract the birds had taken kept some of the language alive and Maya enjoyed listening to them gossip and squabble in the mornings with her tea. When she was in her true dinosaur form, she sometimes answered them, or scared them witless and quiet.

She chuckled. *More often the latter than the former.*

Maya had evolved, too. It had been strange to wake up in a smaller body, one with delicate skin that burned in the sun. She'd panicked at first, desperate to find her original form. It had taken her days to calm down enough to access the part of herself that would always be a large and in charge Maiasaur with olive green, leathery skin striped in cream.

Thank the ManyGods for that.

She'd been in her human guise for roughly five hundred years and she'd seen a lot of shit come her way. Which was why she'd settled in Deadman when she'd had the chance and staked her claim on her land.

And the town came by its name honestly.

The first white man who'd shown up on her land had tried to use her for his sexual needs without her consent and ended up crushed, broken in more places than he had bones, and draped over a boulder as a warning to others.

She snorted. They named the town after him and for at least a century, he'd served as a warning that men had better take heed and be on their best behavior when visiting. Maya honestly hadn't meant to kill him, but she'd shifted when her emotions got the better of her and slammed him into a rock wall before she stepped on him. It had been an accident, but she didn't regret his passing.

Good riddance to bad rubbish.

"Hey, Mom, did you see the news this morning? They're having a public meeting in town on Thursday."

Quinn, her adopted human daughter, strode out to the front deck and plopped down on the nearest chair. Maya marveled at how light humans were. She'd built all her furniture to withstand the density of her own heavier frame, and she had to be careful how she sat so things wouldn't break. But Quinn and Bailey, her adopted human son, could throw themselves onto anything.

Maya focused on Quinn's face, her mammalian features full of irritation. "A public meeting about what?"

Quinn frowned, her cute, freckled nose wrinkling. "It's to see if the residents of Deadman want that tool Clifford Krassobaki to come in here and buy up all the land to make a gawd-awful resort for his ultra-wealthy, tax-evading buddies."

Maya blinked. "Wait...I know I haven't been up on politics and local issues as much as you, but when did this come about?" She set her tea down on the arm of the chair and sat up as Quinn handed her the newspaper, a relict that Quinn still read even though she had an online subscription.

"It's a relatively recent development that started at last month's city council meeting." Quinn rolled her eyes. "That douche Mayor Blatherton, who's friends with Krassobaki, proposed the expansion on Krassobaki's already palatial ranch. They scheduled a public meeting on Thursday to see what the public has to say."

"Oh, I have a lot to say. That would put The Fossil Beds B&B out of business. And where are they gonna get all the people to work this monstrosity? The town holds maybe five hundred humans. Oh hell no." Maya rolled to her feet as her daughter beamed.

"I love it when you get a fire lit under your butt." Quinn grinned as she followed Maya into the kitchen of their B&B. "It doesn't happen often, but it's awesome."

"You just say that because you're the firebrand in this family." Maya shook her head, but a smile curled her lips. "And it's a damn good thing. Too many people got comfortable and let shit like this slide. But not me, not now. Where's your brother?"

Quinn shrugged. "He's down at the Deadman Community Center teaching a class on internet scams and red flags."

"Damn. How did I get such awesome kids? One's a political activist and the other is a community servant."

"You got awesome kids because we learned it from you." Quinn wrapped herself around Maya from behind. "Have I told you that I love you, Mom?"

"Not yet." Maya squeezed Quinn's arms gently.

"Well, I do, and without you, I wouldn't be as awesome as I am. So, it's all your fault." Quinn pulled away and grabbed the paper before heading for the scheduling book. "I'm gonna write down the meeting so you don't forget to go."

"As if I could. You'll be coming too, won't you?"

"Oh yeah. I'm not going to give up my chance to point out all the reasons this is stupid for the town and community." Quinn nodded sharply and relief cascaded through Maya.

She could get up in front of the town and say her piece, but she always had more confidence with her forthright daughter in attendance. There was no way on the Many-Gods' green earth she'd allow a business to come in and decimate her livelihood. Her family, and her secret, were too important.

"You gotta be fucking kidding me!"

Persia Walker stared at the online announcement of the public planning commission meeting. It wouldn't be bad if it was in somewhere like wine country in California or near Aspen, Colorado.

But no, the uber wealthy newspaper tycoon wanted to build it in Wyoming, at the foot of Deadman Mountain in Sublette County. The town had a population of five hundred, making it one of the larger settlements in the state, but still not populous enough to support the staff needs of a snooty rich people's resort. It would drive up the property taxes and push out the locals, making it impossible for ordinary people to live there.

As if they haven't already done that to Jackson Hole.

Persia scowled at the announcement, which included a map of the proposed location of the expansion. She traced the West Washakie River until she reached Little Blind Bear Creek and froze. The proposed site would cover not only both sides of the river, but it would encompass all of Blind Bear and Little Blind Bear creeks, decimating the fossil site she'd been guarding for millennia.

"No. No fucking way." She brought out her phone and took a photo, then headed down the sidewalk toward the little café that had the best peppermint tea this side of the Cretaceous.

Once she had her tea, she headed out to the little sitting area in the front and claimed a bench that could take her full, but muted weight. She set her tea down beside her and pulled out her phone. She hadn't spoken to Professor Nozomi Shimizu in a couple of months since the end of last year's field season, but she'd kept the professor appraised of anything going on near the site. She dialed the university and waited to be connected.

Persia sipped her tea and watched the community awaken around her. Fortunately, she had time to organize people to speak up for both the community and the fossils under her care. There was no way they could let this development go forward, despite what the mayor wanted. She was well aware that Mayor Blatherton was best buds with Krassobaki—everyone was. Blatherton had made it a point to show their connection—so the townspeople would be facing a huge advocate of Krassobaki's development.

But there are more of us than there are of them.

The phoneline clicked over and started ringing. Persia waited until someone picked up. "Hello?"

"Hey, Nozomi, it's Persia. Do you have a moment to talk?"

"Persia! Good to hear from you. Yes, I'm in my off hour. What's going on?"

"Have you seen the announcement of a public meeting here in Deadman over a resort expansion? I'll send you a pic." Persia put the call on speaker and opened the text app. "It's scheduled for this Thursday at six thirty pm. Do you think you could make some time to gather a few of the grad students and come down to Deadman for the meeting?"

There was a short silence as Nozomi absorbed the image. "Yeah, I could do that. Why do you need me there? This seems like a Deadman town issue."

"Did you see the map of the proposed expansion? It straddles the West Washakie River to mile marker seventy-seven on Highway 91."

"Mile marker seventy-seven?" Nozomi was silent a bit longer. "The expansion includes all three of our sites as well as one of the Anthropology department's sites."

"Yup. And if they put that awful resort in there, all those sites will be destroyed for a rich man's vanity and friends."

"Oh hell no. That's not happening. I'll gather who I can, especially Professor Campbell, and we'll be there. Six-thirty on Thursday, you said?"

"Yup. I'm going to let the folks at Friends of Deadman Paleo know as well. I figure if we get enough people there, the project will be dead in the water."

Nozomi sighed through the phone. "I hope so, but as you've said many times, people are very susceptible to money."

"Yeah, but they also like the preserve things and this expansion will hurt their livelihoods and shove them out of their homes. A spark is all it takes to get the community to stand up for their natural resources and way of living."

I hope. She'd seen humans vote against their basic needs because of a promise of money. But she also saw humans cave to a minority when it got loud enough. *We'll just have to be louder.*

"I hope you're right. Okay, let me make some calls and I'll text you when we're on our way on Thursday."

"Sounds good. Thanks, Nozomi." Persia's gullet settled for the first time that morning. "Talk to you on Thursday."

She ended the call and shoved the phone into her back pocket as she let her shoulders relax. There was hope. Not all the humans were money-grubbing, backstabbing bastards. She'd met quite a few who were great beings over the millennia. But she didn't truly trust them until they stood up for things. But Nozomi Shimizu had earned her trust over and over again with her patient and careful exhumation of Persia's sisters from the mudstone near the West Washakie River.

Persia's throat closed as she thought of the members of her herd who'd perished in the mudslide that had come off the hills after several days of rain inundated the area around the watering hole. The clay had been sticky that day and Persia hadn't wanted to stand in it, so she'd retreated into the Gingko trees with several others in her herd to sip water off the leaves of the low-lying shrubs. That was the only thing that had saved them—they were just outside the reach of the wall of mud and vegetation churning in a massive flood. She hadn't realized her sisters were buried until the roar of the muddy maelstrom had filled the river.

And I kept watch over you all these millennia.

She swallowed the lump in her throat as the sorrow hit her again. Usually she carried it with aplomb, not too bothered by it. But the idea that her sisters' resting place would be desecrated by the humans' earthmoving machines to make way for a sunning patio called Dinosaur Reach or something was abhorrent.

Nope, nope, nope.

Persia swallowed the last of her tea and pulled out her phone. Time to call the Friends of Deadman Paleo and the Fossil Beds B&B to set aside some rooms for the folks from the university.

CHAPTER TWO

M aya waited for Quinn and Bailey outside the city
hall and the atmosphere was carnival-like. Despite the subject of the meeting, everyone seemed in high spirits. It was nice to see neighbors and friends gathering in anticipation of the county commissioner's meeting. Mrs. Ledbetter who owned the Sunnyside Up Baker waved at Maya as she headed into the building. Maya loved her zucchini bread muffins with a passion.

The mayor and some of his cronies had snuck in from the back of the building, not willing to face the crowd outside. Typical of Blatherton. He'd been a coward since he was a child bully. She was sure he'd bullied some of the councilpersons into approving Krassobaki's appeal, but the county commissioner, Thomas Stone, hadn't caved to whatever Blatherton threatened and instead called the public meeting.

Smart man, Mr. Stone.

The warm evening air curled around Maya's body and she tipped her head back to take a deep breath. A subtle scent tickled her nose. It smelled of sun-warmed stone, fresh water, and water lilies. Maya dropped her chin and focused on the people around her as a pleasant and soothing vibration hit her breastbone.

Someone important is here.

She'd felt that kind of vibration before, when she found her kids. They'd been on the streets, but their innate kindness and strength had called to her and before she knew it, she was a mom. The same sort of vibration radiated from the people in front of the Deadman City Hall. She stood up on her tiptoes, as the humans liked to call it, looking for the source of the beguiling vibration, but there were too many people in the way.

Quinn and Bailey pushed their way through the crowd toward her and she snorted. It must have been them she sensed. She grinned and opened her arms as her kids closed in on her. While most people gave them amused looks, she hugged her daughter and son as if she hadn't seen them in weeks, rather than hours. She liked the human need for contact and she employed it every chance she got.

"How did it go?" She stood back to look at them.

"Great!" Bailey high-fived her. "We passed out all our flyers and even found people who weren't planning to come to the meeting. We should have a full house tonight."

"And bonus, all the folks who are coming from the university are staying at the B&B." Quinn nodded with satisfaction.

"As they should," Maya agreed.

"Damn straight. Let's go in. I want to get a good seat to watch this tonight." Quinn hooked her arm through Maya's and they all went inside to find a place to sit for the meeting.

Maya noted most of the people at the meeting were either business owners or conservationists, but she also noted that Thomas Stone stood with several other council members away from Mayor Blatherton, their expressions intense and focused.

The soothing vibration hit Maya again and she glanced around, but Bailey settled in the chair beside her, his expression excited and expectant. She frowned a little because while it was similar to her kids' energy, this vibration felt different, yet familiar. Not mammalian at all, but with the same feeling of rightness.

Could there be someone like me here?

The idea sparked both hope and trepidation in her chest. She'd been so sure she was the only one of her kind. In Wyoming at least, but possibly in the world. She'd mostly accepted it as her lot in life—she had no idea how she became who she was now, but she'd resigned herself to being alone. But the idea that there might be someone else like her, and there in Deadman as well, made excitement flutter in her chest.

But who is it?

She let her gaze slide around the room, looking for someone new and different. Most of the people in the room were mammalian.

Although, Blatherton is completely reptilian, and not in a good way.

But she couldn't see anyone she didn't know who *wasn't* mammalian. She didn't know the folks from the university, but she wouldn't see them until that night when they checked in. She was grateful they would stay the night because their bookings would take care of the bills for the month, and it wasn't even the weekend yet.

Finally, the council members took their seats with Commissioner Stone seated in the center and the mayor over to the side. While he had pushed for the expansion, he still had to contend with the public's opinions. Another man, this one as snake-like as Blatherton, wearing an expensive suit, ostrich skin cowboy boots, and a brand-new white Stetson hat, stood just to the side of the meeting area, watching but not engaging.

Could you brown-nose a little more there, buddy?

"I call this meeting to order. Tonight, we're all here to discuss the possibility of permitting the expansion and construction of Clifford Krassobaki's estate into the Western Washakie Resort." Commissioner Stone kept his expression stoic while murmurs circulated through the crowd. "As proposed, the new resort will take up the space between the town limits along Highway 91 and the Deadman Creek, including Blind Bear and Little Blind Bear Creeks, and Mr. Krassobaki's current landholdings in the southeastern quadrant. We'd like to open up the floor to public comment right now. Please state your name, if you're for or against the permit, and a brief explanation as to why. Each speaker will have three minutes to say their piece and the moderator will keep you on time, so don't palaver. All right? Who's our first speaker?"

Several people got to their feet, but they were courteous and eventually worked out who would comment first. There were a couple folks who were in favor of the expansion, saying it could bring in jobs for construction, landscaping, and service. But most people who spoke, while respectful, pointed out why it wasn't a good idea.

When it was Maya's turn, she stood before the podium without a smile. "My name is Maya Sorino and I own and operate the Fossil Beds Bed and Breakfast here in town. I'm against the expansion. Not only will it harm our town in terms of bringing in too many people for the municipal services—where are all the people who have to work at the resort going to live? Jackson?—it will also hurt my business. I depend on the tourists who come to Deadman for hiking, hunting, and our annual festivals, most of which will be curtailed with that much land in private hands. And if these folks go to the resort, I'll lose my livelihood, and I've been here since the town incorporated."

"As if anyone would waste their time at a tiny B&B instead of a nice resort." Krassobaki's grumble reached Maya's ears.

She shot a look at him where he watched the proceedings with a smirk on his face. She narrowed her eyes and he blinked then blanked his expression when he realized she'd heard him.

"I live in this town and I know the businesses here. I also know the people. Mr. Krassobaki isn't our kind of people. He wouldn't help our town, he just wants to own it. Please do not allow this expansion. Thank you."

Maya nodded to Commissioner Stone and returned to her seat as a few others got up. She was shaking with adrenaline and anger. Krassobaki's blatant disregard for the people of her town pissed her off and she hoped the commissioner and the council voted to nix his hideous resort.

"Way to go, Mom." Bailey leaned over and hugged her shoulders. "I was watching the council and they were moved by your words."

"Thanks. I hope it's enough."

The last group of people to get up were from the University of Wyoming, led by a slender, woman of Japanese heritage. She smiled at the committee and straightened her shoulders as she laid her hands on the podium. She was joined by a white woman with curly red hair pulled back into a ponytail and graying at the temples. They gave eloquent speeches on why it was a bad idea to expand the resort because of the historical significance, between the paleontological and anthropological sites along the West Washakie River.

"If you allow this expansion, these sites will be lost to looters and destruction. Please do not allow it. Thank you."

The folks from the University sat down and another woman walked to the podium.

"Who's that?" Quinn pointed to the woman who had her brown hair shaved along the sides of her head to emphasize the rounded mohawk held in place by brightly colored hair bands.

"I don't know. I haven't seen her around before." Maya wished she could see her better, but the woman's back was to the audience.

"Good evening, my name is Persia Walker. I'm the coordinator of Friends of Deadman Paleo and a resident of Deadman, Wyoming. I'm sure you all know me from my determined efforts to preserve the natural treasures of this part of Wyoming." There was a rumble of amusement in the crowd. "Yeah, I know. But hey, y'all got some great scientific history parks out of the deal and now your kids know more paleo than the average dinosaur-loving eight-year-olds."

The laughter turned real and Maya joined in, charmed by Persia's humor.

"I'm here, much like most of the folks and the scientific community from the University of Wyoming, to protest this expansion. We have a rich history here in Deadman—from the moment the town incorporated, there's been hunting, hiking, camping, cross-country skiing opportunities close to our town. Plus, there's the extensive paleontological sites all around. This expansion would not

only decimate those sites, as the University folks pointed out, the construction would disturb the peace with
noise pollution and disrupt the migratory patterns of our
wildlife."

Persia paused and her eyes widened. "And also, where
would the resort get their power? Our substation couldn't
handle their needs. That would require another substation
at least, if not the construction of a power plant or a wind
turbine farm. There's a lot more to consider than just the
resort. I like our town the way it is and I urge y'all to vote
no on the expansion. Thank you."

She turned to sit down and Maya froze. Not only was
Persia the source of the delicious vibration that called to
Maya, but she was also non-human. Specifically, dinosaur
non-human. Maya's heart damn near shot out of her chest.

I'm not alone!

She wished the other woman would make eye contact
with her, but Persia returned to her place with the other
university attendees and the meeting resumed. Maya tried
to pay attention to the way the vote went and the verdict,
but her mind and gaze were locked on the beautiful mohawked woman near the back of the room.

"And the motion carries."

A cheer went up around her and Bailey thumped her on
the shoulder. "Congratulations, Mom! We did it!"

"What?" Maya blinked in confusion.

"We did it! The permit for expansion was denied." Quinn grinned. "Krassobaki can't build or expand. He's SOL!"

"Oh, right. Excellent. I'm so pleased."

Quinn raised an eyebrow and tilted her head. "Weren't you paying attention? Where's your mind at?"

"Sorry, I was distracted." She rose with them and craned her neck to look for Persia Walker, but she couldn't see her in the crowd.

"Yeah, I guess so. Did you see Krassobaki's expression? He could've spit nails." Quinn laughed. "Blatherton was much better, though he was doing some serious ass-kissing, but Krassobaki was having none of it. It was awesome. Twenty bucks says he loses the next election."

"Yeah, because his best buddy isn't gonna fund his campaign." Bailey smirked. "Come on, we better get back to the B&B before the crowd descends for the after party."

Maya jerked in surprise. "After party? What after party?"

"Come on, Mom. You know the university folks are staying the night so they don't have to drive back to Jackson Hole tonight, right? I bet they'll be celebrating hardcore. I've heard geologists know what makes the bedrock." He winked as Maya groaned.

"So many beds, so little time." Quinn smirked as she high-fived her brother.

"You kids are terrible." She mock-scowled at them as she followed them out of the city hall where the jubilant crowd flooded the streets. "My goodness, these folks are thrilled."

"We won a big battle. Did you hear what Commissioner Stone said at the end? It was epic." Bailey's grin widened.

"No, I missed it. What did he say?"

"He said, 'Some things aren't for sale, including our town and me. I'm not for sale, either. Your wealth doesn't mean you can railroad our town, Mr. Krassobaki. Permit denied.'" Bailey shook his head. "It was a beautiful thing. We all cheered."

Maya blew out a sigh of relief. "I'm glad we turned him down, but you know how these ultra-rich folks are. We'll have to keep an eye on him for a little while because he's used to getting what he wants with all that money."

Quinn scowled. "Yeah, but only Blatherton likes him, and no one's particularly fond of Blatherton, so..."

"Yeah, just don't think Krassobaki will be so easily thwarted. I know his type."

They piled into the B&B's pickup and headed back to their place. Maya tried to keep her attention on the kids and the road, but her mind held an image of a beautiful woman who'd spoken about the paleo sites.

"Hey, did you see the woman with the mohawk?" She tried to make it sound casual.

"Persia Walker? Yeah, I did. What about her?" Quinn smirked a little.

"She was with the university folks, wasn't she?"

Bailey shook his head. "Nope. I mean, I think she works with them because she heads Friends of Deadman Paleo, but she lives here in Deadman. Why?"

"Oh." Disappointment cascaded through Maya. "I thought she'd be staying at the B&B with them tonight."

Bailey and Quinn shared a look. "I don't know, Mom. She might be, though I think she lives in town."

It was just as well. What would Maya say to Persia anyway? *Hey, I noticed you've got a bigger vibration than the body you're wearing. Been in town for the last few million years?* Yeah, that probably would do nothing but make Persia either run or ask if Maya was seeing a whole tribe of psychiatrists.

And this is Wyoming—you don't know if she's queer friendly.

Back in her time, things had been simpler. Relationships between beings hadn't been so gender restrictive. Granted, the only way Maya could have eggs was to find a male to mate with, but maiasaurs didn't mate with the same male each season. The only long-term relationships she had were with her female herdmates. They had each other's backs and helped raise the little ones.

Some males always hung around, and they often protected the herd from the bigger predators, but they came and went. The females always stayed together. Maya missed her sister herd, but maybe she'd found a former member. Maybe they could share memories over tea.

They pulled into the garage at the B&B, Bailey and Quinn chattering about the meeting and the town's win over big money. Maya hoped they were right as she followed them inside. She headed into the kitchen to start the oven for the vegetarian lasagna she'd prepared earlier.

The kids went on into the building to check the rooms for the coming guests without being asked. Maya smiled to herself as she set the kettle on the stove. She had the best kids, even if they were mammalian. Best decision she'd made when she rescued them.

Now if she could just find a smart woman to connect with, life would be perfect.

A smart woman like Persia Walker.

"Come on, Persia. Join us for dinner at the B&B. Our treat." Nozomi wrapped an arm around Persia's waist and squeezed gently. "We'd love to have you help us celebrate our win."

Despite Persia's long day getting everything and everyone organized for the meeting, she really wanted to visit the Fossil Beds B&B, but not to celebrate the win over Krassobaki. She desperately wanted to talk to the gorgeous owner.

Maya Sorino.

She loved the name the moment she heard it. It rang in her head like the trumpeting call of her sisters, those beloved herdmates she'd lost all those millions of years ago.

My sisters, who these university humans are digging up.

But Nozomi and her students treated the bones with the utmost love and respect, and Persia was glad her sisters were getting recognition. While she still ached for their loss, she'd found solace in the humans' love for them.

There was something about Maya, though. Something beguiling, like a familiar tune just out of hearing. Persia could sense the sounds, but she couldn't hear them clearly. She had the distinct feeling if she spoke to Maya, the sounds would make sense.

"Are you sure? I don't want to impose, and I've got stuff at home." She tried to give them an out even if she desperately wanted to join them.

"Absolutely. You were a big part of this fight, and you deserve to celebrate. Come with us to the B&B." Nozomi gave her a brilliant smile. "See if you can keep up with the geologists when we party."

Persia snorted. "Been there, done that, got the T-shirt." But she climbed into the van with the rest of the university crew and settled in for the short drive to the B&B.

When they arrived, all the lights were on in the adorable, log cabin-style house. The few tall pine trees Deadman boasted seemed to have congregated around the B&B. The driveway was long and wide for easy maneuvering and someone had built a portico over the entrance for easy drop off. They stopped under the portico to unload before the driver found a place to park. Persia went with them through the thick, wood door with a diamond shaped window at head-height, and stopped inside the entrance.

The foyer of the Fossil Beds B&B had the classic log cabin look with thick beams made of whole tree trunks stained and polished to a high shine. Everything glowed with a golden light and large potted plants like palms, monstera leaf plants, and elephant ears, stood around the foyer. It looked like a warm, inviting, tropical forest, and

Persia had a flash back to when she and her sisters had wandered around the inland sea. Her throat closed for a moment and she blinked back tears.

"Welcome to the Fossil Beds Bed & Breakfast. Can I get your names to verify your reservation?" The young woman with light brown eyes and honey brown hair smiled at them.

"Oh yes, of course. I'm Professor Nozomi Shimizu and this is Professor Audrey Campbell from the University of Wyoming. These are our students. I believe we have a reservation for one night?" Nozomi strode up to what looked like a writing desk with a computer, phone, and payment apparatus.

The young woman nodded and clicked away at the computer. "Ah, yes. I see you have two rooms reserved. Good thing, because this weekend is the Highland Games in Jackson and we get full in a hurry." She clicked a couple of things. "You're all checked in. If I can verify your vehicle license plate number, make and model, I'll get your keys."

Persia left the university folks to get settled and wandered around the B&B house. She found a library space with a big fireplace and lots of windows to let in the natural light. More plants decorated the corners near bookshelves full of books on various subjects, including a sizable selection of paleontological texts.

"This used to be the parlor of the original house, but no one has simple sit-downs anymore."

Persia turned and found the beautiful woman she'd seen at the public meeting leaning against the doorway. Her heart beat an excited tattoo against her ribs as she took in Maya Sorino, proprietor of the Fossil Beds B&B.

She's not human.

No, she was like Persia in some way, though perhaps not the same species. Persia recognized the scent of a dinosaur shifter, but Maya smelled different from the scents of Persia's sisters. Persia didn't really care which species Maya belonged to. She was just happy to discover she wasn't alone anymore.

"Uh, yeah. What's up with that? Who doesn't like a good sit-down?" Persia tried to remember where she was as she stepped forward, holding out her hand. "Persia Walker, head of Friends of Deadman Paleo."

Maya grasped her palm and squeezed gently. "Yes, I saw you at the meeting. Maya Sorino, owner of the Fossil Beds B&B. It's very nice to meet you. How long have you been in Deadman?"

Persia didn't want to let go, so she held Maya's hand as she shrugged. "Not too long. Just a couple of decades." *Yeah, twenty-one of them.* "I thought I knew everyone in

Deadman, but I'm ashamed to admit I haven't seen you before. Have you always owned this place?"

Maya nodded, still holding Persia's hand as if she didn't want to let go. "I have. It wasn't always called the Fossil Beds B&B. We only converted it into a bed and breakfast nine years ago, and then the pandemic hit." She shrugged. "You know how that goes. I became a damn hermit, but at least I had all this space to enjoy. My library grew substantially in the last few years. Thank the ManyGods for online bookstores."

Persia turned her head to look around, enjoying not only the contact with Maya but the full shelves around them. "It's a great library. So much better than a parlor, in my opinion."

Maya nodded and released Persia's hand. Persia immediately missed the contact.

"I think most people tend to use coffee shops for that nowadays, although a few of our guests have whiled away a day in here." Maya gave her a smile. "So, what brings you here tonight? Are you staying?"

Persia shook her head. "No, I live in town, but my friends from the university invited me to dinner with them tonight. Is that okay? I don't want to get in the way."

"Oh, no, we have plenty of food. Huge salad, vegetarian lasagna, rolls, steamed broccoli, and green tea sorbet for dessert." Maya gestured further down the hallway. "Come with me to the kitchen and I'll show you the spread."

Persia trailed after her, enjoying both the energy in Maya's home but also Maya's swaying ass encased in denim capris.

Stop drooling—that's for ankylosaurs!

They entered a beautiful kitchen with wide counters, a big island full of cupboards, and gleaming appliances. The place smelled like delicious baked goods and lasagna, and Persia's mouth watered again.

"Wow, this house is beautiful. I love the stone counters. Are they locally sourced?"

Maya beamed as she pulled out plates for a buffet-style serving. "If 'local' means the whole US, then yes, though that was one of the recent upgrades we made to the house. This quartzite comes from Idaho, but I loved the honey color so much that I couldn't resist."

"I can see why."

Maya beamed. "Come, serve yourself and get here before the herd." She tilted her head. "Unless you'd like me to serve you?"

Heat surged through Persia and made her cheeks prickle as she thought about the kind of service she'd really like.

Jeez, mind out of the gutter, Persia! You don't even know if she's into women.

Although, the way Maya was looking at her, Persia suspected she was wrong. And strictly speaking, neither of them were actually women, in the human sense of the word.

She cleared her throat. "Uh, no, I'm good. Thank you for the supper. It smells delicious."

Maya shrugged modestly. "It's good to have adult company. My kids are awesome, but we talk about kid things like school and local events. It's very nice to meet someone new, especially someone like you."

Persia took her time filtering through the meanings of Maya's words. "Someone like me?"

Maya shot a look around to be sure no one stood near them, but still lowered her voice. "Someone...prehistoric."

To anyone else, it would sound like an agism insult, but Persia understood completely and her lips curled into a smile.

"Let me guess. You're prehistoric, too?"

Maya's smile warmed Persia from the inside out. "Yes. It's been so long since I've seen anyone of my own kind. I didn't know anyone lived in Deadman, besides me."

"Well, I don't actually live *in* Deadman. I have a cabin just outside the city limits because of the...roaming capabilities." She'd learned a long time ago to use euphemisms around humans and old habits died hard.

"Oh goodness. You don't live anywhere near that douchebag Krassobaki, do you?" Maya shot her an aghast look as she served up two plates Persia assumed were for her kids.

"No, not quite, though if he'd gotten permission to expand, we would've been neighbors."

And wouldn't have that been a helluva a thing?

His guests would have seen a monster moving around in the distance and fucked up her life more than she wanted.

"Ugh. That guy gives me the creeps. Plus, he'd ruin our town and our homes. I'm so glad he lost the vote tonight."

Before Persia could answer, the kitchen filled with the folks from the university and Maya turned into a hostess. She greeted everyone, explained the buffet, and made sure everyone had drinks. Persia accepted a cup of tea while the geologists all went for beer or wine. The conversation shifted to the meeting that night and how they'd won a victory against entitled wealth.

While Persia laughed and shared with the group, she couldn't help the feeling that Krassobaki wasn't done yet. Something about the guy reminded her of a wily Sarcosuchus waiting in the shallows for his time to strike. But she tried to smile and relax for the moment with her friends, celebrating their small victory.

CHAPTER THREE

T he university people were hilarious and great company. Both Bailey and Quinn joined them for dinner, and there was a lively discussion about science, paleo, archeology, and politics. Maya loved the quiet confidence of Professor Shimizu and the forthrightness of Professor Campbell. Their students ranged everywhere between, and Maya's kids held their own as they celebrated.

But mostly, Maya watched Persia. She'd know Persia was important the moment she saw her, and Maya wanted more time with the attractive dinosaur shifter. She loved the way Persia had shaved the sides of her head to emphasize her mohawk, like she was showing off a crest.

Oooh, is that indicative of her dinosaur form?

Maya was a *Maiasauria peeblesorum* with more of a parrot's beak than a duckbill, and glorious pale cream stripes across her back, down her tail, and around both hind legs. Her skin was a deep olive green that darkened to nearly black on her legs. Besides the cream stripes, her eyes glowed gold in the light.

Her human form had taken some of those qualities. She had golden olive skin, dark hair, and light brown eyes that resembled the color of her dinosaur form. Persia, in contrast, had creamy pale skin, black hair with blue stripes in it, and brown eyes with so much russet in them they appeared red in certain light.

So which species is she?

Maya's memories of the world back 65 million years ago were a little hazy. There were plenty of tiny dinosaurs wandering around in the shrubbery when she was a kid, and the bigger herbivores—Stegosaurus, Triceratops, Pachycephalosaurus, Parasaurolophus, Iguanodon, Apatosaurus, Brachiosaurus, Chasmosaurus and Styracosaurus—had often traveled with her herd of Maiasaurs.

Maya squinted as she sat back in her chair. *If I had to guess—and I do—I'd say Persia is a Hadrosaur of some kind.*

That felt right and more excitement poured into Maya's system.

What if she's a Maiasaur like me?

She shivered as Persia met her gaze and the connection seemed electric. Maya hadn't figured out who she wanted to mate with when she'd only been in her true form, but over the years as a human, she'd always been more attracted to women than men. That night, sitting in her home with Persia, she wanted the blue-haired, creamy skinned woman like she'd wanted no other in all her millennia.

But they had other guests, plus her kids, so there wasn't any time to do much more than socialize and eat. The university folks were fun and full of stories of camping in the rain, strange beings seen while out on digs, and that one time a set of mountain goats ran away with their boots. Maya hadn't laughed so hard in forever, and it was a good night.

Eventually, the university folks cried off and started heading to bed. Maya got her kids situated for bedtime, too, sending them upstairs to get any last homework done. She began packing up the leftover food and Persia joined her. While Maya packed up the food, Persia scraped the plates, rinsed them, and loaded the dishwasher. It was the most domestic interaction she'd had with Persia, and it felt completely natural, as if they'd done it a hundred times.

"Thanks for having me over for supper. It was great." Persia put the soap in the dishwasher and started it. "I guess I should get going."

"Are you sure?" Maya bit her lip at the pleading tone to her voice. "I mean, I'm delighted you were here to share in dinner and if you have some extra time, I'd love to spend more with you." *Please don't let her leave yet.*

Persia paused in the hallway to the front door. "Are *you* sure? I know you've had a long day and now you have guests. I don't want to take up too much of your time."

"Please take up some of my time." Maya grinned. "I can't tell you how good it is to find someone like me. I thought I was the only one, and while humans are nice, they'll never understand what it's like to be Prehistoric among the modern."

Persia snorted softly. "Yeah, it's amazing how short-sighted they are, even those with their eyes on the past." She nodded her head toward the ceiling. "I like Professor Shimizu, but she only knows a little about me."

"Right. So, if you have time, do you want to...I don't know, take a walk or something?" Maya gestured to the door. "We could walk the nature trail through the forest. It doesn't go very far, but there's a nice view about halfway up."

"Yeah, okay. I'd like that." Persia opened the door and held it for Maya to step through. "I promise to have you home by curfew."

Maya barked a laugh. "I don't even know what that means in terms of Prehistoric beings."

"Pretty much next to nothing, but it made you laugh, so win for me." Persia closed the door behind her and waited for Maya to lock it before stepping off the front porch. "Where's the trail?"

"This way."

Maya headed around the north side of the house along a path she'd paved with chunks of local silt stone. Quinn had helped her install native plants and grasses that would bloom throughout the year and provide food for pollinators. The path always felt soothing to her, but with Persia's company, it felt magical.

I found another being like me.

Delight ran through her as they traversed around the house and stepped through the rough-hewn gate at the back of the property. She wanted to show Persia everything wonderful about her place, in all times of day and all seasons. Now that she'd met Persia, Maya knew she'd made a life-long friend, and hopefully more.

If *Persia is into women.*

Which she still hadn't verified. Not that it was easy in Wyoming, where the social mores of humans baffled her. Why they were so afraid of non-mating couples, she'd never understand. Maya didn't want to lose the connection with Persia yet, so she didn't ask the question as they hiked through the nighttime forest.

"It's really beautiful out here. I haven't hiked Deadman Mountain before." Persia's voice held wonder and her expression matched.

Thank goodness I can see in the dark better than humans.

"It is. It's one of my favorite places here and why I built my home near it." Maya paused before the big reveal and held out her hand. "Ready for a surprise?"

Persia took her hand. "Yup."

They stepped out of the trees to a cleared overlook. The lights of the B&B sat directly below them and the town spread out in a glitter mosaic up the length of the valley.

"Whoa."

The amazement in Persia's voice warmed Maya all the way to her bones. She let the other woman step ahead to get the full expanse of the view. Moonlight painted the West Washakie River silver and the forest around the town deep blue. The lights of town offered a glittering contrast and made a scenic fairytale.

"This is amazing."

Maya nodded. "You should see it in the fall. All the aspens shift in color and it looks like huge swaths of gold have hit the town."

"I would like to see that." Persia shot her a warm smile. "So, have you always lived in Deadman?"

Maya shook her head. "I'm originally from Montana, up near Kalispell, but when I woke up in my new body, I headed south out of the harsher winters. Montana can suck the heat right out of you."

"Yeah, it can. I'm actually from South Dakota originally, but my family migrated down here to the West Washakie in the winters. SoDak is the same as Montana and, except for the Black Hills, there are no trees to stop the wind." Persia shivered theatrically. "Wyoming gets pretty cold, but not like the Dakotas."

"Yeah, I don't mind the winters, though I like them better in my human form. So many ways to keep warm nowadays." Maya bit her lip and tried to think of something other than small talk. "Persia, can I ask you a personal question?"

Persia's expression turned amused. "Sure."

"Let me preface this by saying I'm so glad I've met you, and I'm delighted to find someone like me in Deadman—I honestly thought I was the only one. But..." She trailed off as she took courage from the view ahead of them. "I wanted to know if you'd like to get together for coffee or dinner or something regularly? I, uh, I really like spending time with you, even though I just met you tonight."

Persia's smile widened. "I'd like that a lot. In fact, I was working up the courage to ask you out. I know you have a family and a business that takes up a lot of your time, but I really like being with you, and would like to spend more time with you."

"Really?" Maya blushed and cleared her throat. "Sorry, I sound like a teenager with her first crush, and technically, you *are* my first crush since I woke up in this body. Not that I'm crushing on you, per se, just that—"

Persia grabbed Maya's lapels and pulled her close to plant a kiss on her lips, effectively stopping the flow of words. She tasted of the meal they'd eaten and dark spice straight from a mineral hot springs. Maya fell into the kiss, moaning in both relief and delight. Their tongues tangled and arousal shot straight down to her core. Her nipples tightened in her shirt and she rubbed them against Persia's chest to relieve the ache.

When they broke apart, Persia's cheeks were flushed and her eyes glittered in the light of the moon.

"I like being your first crush. For the record, you're the first being I've been attracted to since my herdmates died."

It took a few moments for Maya's brain to catch up with the words. "Oh. Oh! You lost your herd? I'm so sorry. That must have been awful."

Persia shrugged and looked away for a moment. "It's been a very long time. But Professor Shimizu and her students are digging them up and preserving them, so they'll be honored."

"What?" Maya blinked. "Oh, my goodness! The paleo dig is of your herdmates?"

Persia nodded. "Yes, and the only reason I'm letting them do the dig is because they will honor the bones as they should."

"Wow." Maya reached out and grasped Persia's hand. "I'm so sorry for your loss, but I'm very glad you survived and I got to meet you, here, now, in this era. Have you been alone all this time?"

Persia grimaced. "Not always alone, but apparently we're rare, us Prehistoric beings, and finding someone who not only understood me, but was my type, was something of a challenge."

"Oh, I understand that completely. Humans are crazy judgmental for having such short lives."

Persia snorted. "Judgmental, destructive, and value money and gold over the important things like family and herd."

Maya sighed. "Yeah, I've heard it termed 'wetiko.' A disease of feeling they never have enough. I think Clifford Krassobaki suffers from it."

"Hmm, I wouldn't be surprised. He's a snake. I don't think tonight's setback will stop him for long." Persia scowled and let her gaze slide back to the view, but didn't let go of Maya's hand. "I have the feeling he's going to do something destructive, as humans will, to get his way. The old 'if-I-can't-have-it-no-one-can' routine."

Maya's heart sank. "You think so?"

Persia nodded. "But we'll stop him. We just need to keep an eye on him for a little while." She squeezed Maya's hand. "In the meantime, I'd like to spend more time with you. I know you're very busy with your B&B, but maybe you can add me to your schedule?"

Maya's heart fluttered with excitement and hope. "Really? I mean, absolutely, I can add you to my schedule. I'll *make* time to be with you. It's worth it to me."

"Yeah? Good." Persia leaned into Maya and brushed her lips with a gentle kiss. "It's worth it to me, too." She pulled back and grinned. "Now, let me walk you home, young lady."

Maya laughed. "How 'bout I walk you to your car? And please text me when you get home so I know you made it safely."

Persia raised an eyebrow as they turned to head down the trail. "I don't have your number."

Maya yanked out her phone and opened the contacts app. "What is yours? I'll text you and you'll have mine." There was no way she'd let Persia leave without getting her number. Just because she was Prehistoric didn't mean she couldn't keep up with technology.

Persia rattled off her number and Maya sent her a little dinosaur emoji in a text. Persia chuckled as she checked her phone.

"Perfect, now I can text you anytime I want."

Maya nodded. "Exactly."

Persia shoved her phone into her back pocket and grasped Maya's hand with a smile. "One thing I like about the human body is the hands. Makes it easy to touch without impeding movement."

Maya couldn't stop the smile from stretching her lips as she nodded. They didn't say anything more as they continued down the trail, listening to the night sounds in the forest and enjoying each other's silent companionship. They came to the gate and stepped through, Maya scanning her home for anything amiss. Not that she expected anything, but the energy of the public meeting still made her nervous. It was like their town was holding its breath, waiting for something to happen.

Me, too.

When they arrived at the front, Maya realized Persia had come with the university folks and didn't have a way back to town.

"I guess I'm walking." Persia gave her a shrug. "Thanks for dinner and the hike. Both were great."

"Oh, my goodness. I can't let you *walk* home. You can stay here for the night. There are plenty of rooms and we don't fill up until tomorrow night anyway." Maya caught Persia's arm and squeezed.

"No, it's okay. I don't want to impose or be in your space too much. I don't want you to get tired of me. We just met tonight."

"And it feels like we've known each other forever. At least, it does to me." Maya squeezed again before letting go. "I want you to stay, Persia. Spend the night with me. We could just talk, drink peppermint tea, and share stories. Please?"

Persia bit her lip, uncharacteristically hesitant. She didn't want to screw this new friendship up before she'd had a chance to really get to know Maya. But she was being given an opportunity to spend more time with Maya, learning her and protecting her.

Yeah, like I'm some sort of Spinosaur or something.

But she did want to protect Maya, even if Krassobaki was threatening the dig site rather than the B&B.

He definitely is threatening it with a loss of business.

"I want to accept..."

"But?" Maya raised her eyebrows.

"But I really need to get home, clean up my place, do laundry, and keep an eye on the dig site." She tried to soften her refusal with a warm smile. "I would love to stay, but I want to do this right. You're the first being I've met in a long time that makes me want to hang out more, and that's why I don't want to go too fast. Does that make sense?"

"Er, yes, of course." Maya's expression closed down and Persia inwardly groaned. "Can I at least give you a ride to your home so you don't have to walk?"

Persia's first inclination was to decline because she really needed to get her thoughts in order. But a little voice in the back of her head said Maya would take it as another rejection and it could cost her in the long run.

"Yes, please, that would be great. Thank you."

Maya's expression softened into a relieved smile. "Okay, let me just go get my purse."

"A Prehistoric female has a purse?" Dry amusement oozed from Persia's voice.

Maya snorted. "Oh, hell yeah. I'm not a kangaroo—I don't have my own pouch to carry stuff. Just be glad I said no to the Gucci crocodile skin purse someone once tried to give me. It felt too creepy carrying around a suchus relative."

"Ew, yeah. That would be creepy."

Maya hurried into the B&B and came out a few moments later with her keys in her hand. She led Persia over to a forest-green Jeep Cherokee 4x4 and gestured for her to get in. The vehicle had to be over twenty years old, but it purred like a saber-toothed cat when she started it. They didn't talk much on the drive into town other than to share directions to where Persia left her truck, but when they arrived at city hall, she gave Maya a grateful smile.

"Hey, I just wanted to say thanks for dinner and the hike again. I'm so glad I got to meet you and spend some time with you. Can I call you tomorrow?"

Maya nodded. "Sure. Call or text. Either is fine."

She reached out to grasp Maya's arm. "I'm serious about not screwing this up. You're worth all the extra effort, even though we've just met. I'm not going home tonight because I don't want to be with you. I'm going home so I can get my home in order in case you drop by." She grinned. "Can't have you thinking I'm a slob."

Maya laughed, though it sounded a little sad. "We wouldn't want that. Please let me know via text when you make it home, okay? Otherwise, I'll worry."

"Done. Drive safely home, yourself."

Maya nodded and waited for Persia to get to her truck and unlock the doors. Then she waved and headed back out to her B&B. Persia stood and watched her taillights pull away into the darkness. Both went as far as she could see before winking out behind the trees. She sighed and climbed into the driver's seat, wishing she could've stayed with Maya, but knowing she made the right decision to go home.

She made it to her cabin and parked, pausing outside the truck to listen to the forest. Everything looked safe and quiet, and nothing set off any warnings. She headed inside and pulled out her phone to text Maya that she'd made it home. She found one from the other woman already, and she replied with some emojis, including one Parasaurolophus dinosaur.

There, make her guess at my species.

Maya immediately sent back heart emojis along with flowers and the words, "Good night."

Persia didn't have any trouble falling asleep, dreaming of a beautiful woman with honey brown hair and a well-rounded ass.

CHAPTER FOUR

As promised, Persia called the next day after the public meeting, but Maya was so busy cleaning rooms and preparing for the weekend's guests, she didn't have time to call back. Persia offered to help with the B&B's heavy schedule during the Highland Games rush. Maya was delighted and they spent the weekend working and getting to know each other better. Persia even got to know Quinn and Bailey.

She liked Quinn's activist spirit and they compared notes on how to get their elected officials to do the right thing. With Bailey she shared the love of video games—damn, those human artists and programmers came up with the coolest stuff—and teaching others new skills. Bailey's expertise lay with the internet while hers remained with paleo. The kids started calling her Mama Mo for her mohawk, and the nickname warmed her heart.

In the evenings, they'd take walks together, in their human forms, to keep anyone from paying too close attention to them, but Persia ached to show Maya her true form. But they rarely got time alone together with the guests needing towels, food, a random pipe broken in the kitchen, and a lost llama.

How does one lose a freakin' woolly herbivore?

When Maya got really busy, Persia got out of her way by "hiking" around the dig site where her sisters still lay encased in mudstone. Persia always felt peaceful when she spent time there, as if her sisters recognized her presence. A new emotion marred the peace, though, and on Sunday afternoon, Persia sat in the shade of the pines above the gridded space of the dig site, tears streaming down her cheeks.

"So, I've met someone." She spoke aloud, even though their communication had always been with body language and grunts. "She's amazing, and she's one of us. Well, one of the *me* kind of us. I haven't seen her true form yet, but there's a connection I've been missing since I lost you."

She brushed some dirt off her knee as she gathered her thoughts. "Her name is Maya, and she owns the local Bed & Breakfast—not that you'd know what that is, but it's a respectable profession. She has two mammalian children, but it's not a surprise. The mammals have taken over, so we had to adapt. Anyway, I really like her and I'm pretty sure I survived just to meet her."

The wind rattled the aspen leaves and made the pines creak as Persia wrestled with her guilt of moving on from the females she'd loved most. "I don't want you to think I'll ever forget you. In fact, the paleontologists are preserving your bones for others to enjoy your beauty. They're good people and they'll take care of you better than I can."

The energy of the site shifted as if her sisters were forgiving her. "I can't be here all the time and there are too many threats to your resting place. This seemed like the best solution. Tonight, I'm going to bring Maya out here to meet you so she knows who you were to me. I think you'll like her. She makes me really happy. I know it seems sudden and fast, but she gets me just like you did. You know how we just knew? It's the same."

The wind rustled the trees and more of her guilt sloughed away. She rose and brushed the dirt off her ass. "So, yeah, that's just what I wanted to tell you. I'll bring her by tonight so you can see I'm in good hands, okay?" She smiled at the bones in the ground. "I love you. I'll always love you. And when they display the bones in the museum, we'll come by to see you, okay?"

She nodded as the wind made the leaves rustle in acceptance. "Thanks for hearing me out. See you tonight."

Persia waved at the bones and headed back toward the main parking area of the site. Old habits died hard and she scanned the dirt road and clearing for tire tracks that didn't belong. Her gut said Krassobaki wasn't giving up, but she'd been keeping an eye on the site, and nothing seemed out of place. She sniffed the air, searching for scents other than dirt, vegetation, water, and woodland mammals, but nothing came to her nose.

Of course, I'm a little limited in my human form.

Shaking her head, she climbed into her truck and headed back into town to spend time with Maya before their first official date.

"Ooooh, Mom's going on a date!" Bailey grinned and wiggled his fingers at Maya's face. "She's gettin' all gussied up. Check out that eyeshadow. Fresh out of the 1990s, I'm told."

"Shut up, you wouldn't know the 90s if they sauntered by in ripped, acid-washed jeans and a mullet." Quinn snorted as she checked off the departing guests in the computer.

"Mullets were from the 80s, dork." Bailey stuck his tongue out.

"And bell bottoms were from the 70s. What's your point?" Quinn looked down her nose at him.

"My *point* is Mom is still dressing like it's last century."

Maya barely refrained from rolling her eyes. *Just imagine if you saw me in my real form. Then you wouldn't be talking centuries.* But she kept her thoughts off her face and her amusement to herself.

"Last century or this century, I don't think Persia cares. She just likes Mom as she is and I think it's adorable." Quinn beamed as Maya straightened her strappy sundress.

"Thank you, Quinn. I'm glad you approve of Persia because I'm hoping this is the first of many dates." Maya pulled a shawl over her shoulders.

"Really? You think she's the one?" Bailey raised his eyebrows. "Isn't it kinda fast?"

Maya shrugged as she stepped into her Teva hiking sandals. "Sometimes, it doesn't take months or years or decades to know the person is the right one. When you know, you just know. That's the way it is with Persia."

"Does she feel the same, Mom?" Bailey's brows beetled and his mouth tightened.

"I don't know yet, but I think so. Why?"

"Because I don't want you to get hurt." For a moment, he looked as fierce as a Chasmosaurus facing off with a flock of Compsognathus.

She smiled and cupped his cheek. "Hey, I know you're watching out for me, kiddo. But even if Persia doesn't feel the same, I'll be okay. I've got a big heart." *Literally*. "And I have you both in my life. You don't have to worry about me. Okay?"

Bailey grimaced and nodded. "Okay, but I know what it's like to have your heart broken. We both do."

"I know, kiddo. But even if it doesn't work out with Persia, you'll always have me in your corner. I'm not going anywhere, okay?" Maya hugged Bailey. "I got you no matter what."

"Yeah, okay, Mom." He hugged her back before they heard Persia's voice downstairs. "I think she's here."

"Right. How do I look?" Maya straightened her dress and shawl in the mirror one last time.

"You look spectacular." Quinn grinned at her from the mirror. "Don't worry about the B&B. We've got it covered tonight. Just go have fun."

"I will." She headed downstairs.

The vision in the foyer damn near stole her breath.

"Wow."

Persia had dressed in knee-length denim shorts under a white V-necked cotton shirt with brightly colored embroidered flowers at the neck and cuffs. It was opaque enough to hide her areolas despite the nipples pushing against the soft fabric. She'd used gold hairbands to tie up her mohawk, and they glittered in the light.

"Wow? Is that a good wow or an ew wow?"

"Good. Very good." Maya grinned. "The most beautiful woman I've ever seen."

To her surprise, Persia blushed. "Thank you. You look pretty spectacular yourself."

"Thank you." Maya beamed as warmth filled her chest. "I'm so glad you think so. My kids say I'm dressed from the wrong century."

Persia snorted and rolled her eyes. "Just because they can't see our awesomeness doesn't mean we don't. We should probably go before they realize just how amazing we are and mob us like adoring fans."

Maya laughed. "We'll just wave and smile. But yeah, let's beat the rush." She glanced back over her shoulder at Quinn. "I have my keys so you can lock the doors after eleven. Don't wait up for me."

"Okay, Mom. Have fun and be safe."

Maya waved and stepped out the door with Persia behind her, excitement putting a spring into her step. Persia trotted up beside her and opened the truck's passenger side door.

"Where are we going tonight?" Maya climbed into the seat and arranged her skirt over her knees.

"My place. I want to show you something special and it's easier to get there from my yard." Persia closed the door and walked around the hood before she climbed into the driver's seat. "I also thought we'd go for walk au naturel."

Maya raised her eyebrows. "You mean, as in...Prehistoric?"

"Yup." Persia gave her a smug smile. "I want to see your beautiful form in the moonlight."

Heat flushed Maya's face as they drove south of town along the North Deadman Creek. They turned off to the east before they reached the river and the sign for Krassobaki's palatial estate. Maya tried not to grimace, but her face must have ignored her warnings because Persia grunted with amusement.

"I feel the same about that bastard."

"Krassobaki?"

"Yes. I don't think he'll give up without doing something stupid."

They wound through a boulder field on the green hills until they abutted against the forest at the base of Deadman Mountain. A cute A-frame cabin stood in a clearing surrounded by tall ponderosa pines. A wide tributary to Deadman Creek cut through the front of the property with an arching one-car bridge spanning its chuckling waters.

"Wow, this is gorgeous. So peaceful out here." Maya stared in delight at the cabin as Persia parked. "How long have you had this place?"

"I bought it in the early nineteenth century pretending to be a prospector. Built the cabin over time and made upgrades." Persia turned off the engine and got out. "I figured we'd come here first to leave our clothes and pick up my go-bag."

Maya slid out of the vehicle and blinked. "Go-bag?"

"Yeah. I use it when I want to go walking in my true form but need to care shit like my phone, keys, and a bottle of electrolytes. Gotta keep my salts up." She led Maya to the cabin and unlocked the door. "Come on in. If you want to add your phone and keys to the go-bag, it's on the couch."

Persia pointed before she unlaced her sneakers and set them aside. Maya pulled out her phone and keys, and added them to the small, zippered pocket on the duffle bag on the couch. Then she took off her sandals and set the by the door.

"Are we just going to undress here then shift outside?"

"Well, yeah. I mean, I'd prefer my clothes stay dry and safe inside, but I'm too big to shift indoors."

Persia pulled her shirt over her head and laid it on a nearby chair. She wasn't wearing a bra and Maya took a moment to admire Persia's creamy skin with dark cinnamon areolas and nipples. Because they were dinosaur shifters, they didn't have hair on their mounds, but the faint pattern of lighter, slightly shimmery scales graced Persia's pubic area as she shoved her denim shorts off her ass.

"Sweet glory, you're gorgeous." The words snuck out before Maya could stop them, but that didn't make them untrue.

Persia stood up and grinned. "Thank you. Can I see your version?"

A flattered smile curled Maya's lips as she tugged her summer dress off and draped it over the same chair with Persia's clothes. Her scale patch was darker than her golden skin-tone, but her nipples were more dusky rose, a color description she'd seen at the lipstick counter.

"Oh wow, Maya. You're just lovely." Persia sidled up close and ran her hands over Maya's hips. "I love the dark patch between your legs." She shivered. "Makes me think naughty thoughts."

"Oh, yeah?" Maya stroked the flesh between Persia's breasts. "I'm a breast girl. I'm really enjoying the look of yours." She cupped one full breast and let her thumb play over the cinnamon nipple. "Ooh, so responsive."

Persia groaned and stepped back. "I so want to give into whatever is going through your head right now, but I want to take a walk first. Maybe we'll come back here and follow your ideas afterward."

"I'm gonna hold you to that." Maya grinned but waved at the door. "Shall we shift and take our stroll?"

"Yes."

Persia led the way outside and the moonlight caressed her creamy pale skin with its blue light. Maya followed, admiring the play of muscles under Persia's skin. She was so focused, she damn near tripped over her feet going down the stairs of the porch. Persia chuckled and Maya's face flamed, but she got herself under control as they moved away from the house and truck.

Persia glanced over her shoulder but didn't say a word. One moment there was a beautiful naked woman with a blue and gold mohawk and a fine ass, and the next, a glorious Parasaurolophus with blue stripes on mottled gold and black skin with a creamy underbelly running from her chin to the tip of her tail. All in all, she stood roughly sixteen feet high at the shoulder and about thirty-five feet long from nose to tail tip. The moonlight made her stripes glow electric blue and brought out the red in her eyes.

"Wow."

Persia tossed her head and gave a low trumpeting call as if to say, "Get on with it, honey!"

"Oh, right."

Maya started walking and focused on letting her true form out. It felt a little like unzipping a slightly tight, pleather catsuit, and her body took a relieved breath as it filled out its usual dimensions. Walking made it easier to resume her larger form.

She'd never actually taken her measurements, but when she finally strode up beside Persia, she was significantly smaller in height and length. Plus, she didn't have the very cool crest on the back of her head. But she was stouter and more robust than her lovely companion.

Persia rumbled a joyous greeting and rubbed her muzzle against Maya's jaw with affection. The moment they touched, Maya could hear a voice that sounded remarkably like Persia's human voice in the back of her head.

"So beautiful. Oh, your stripes are divine. Like a zebra, only sexier."

Maya froze. *"Persia?"*

Persia lifted her head and focused one eye on Maya. *"Maya...?"*

"Yes, it's me. Can you hear me?" Maya nodded her head.

"Yes, well, not hear so much as understand. How is this happening?" Persia moved around to get a better look at Maya with both eyes.

"I don't know. I've never spoken to someone like you before. When I was last in this form full time, we just used body language and grunts." Maya nuzzled Persia's neck and shoulder, trying to convey comfort. *"I like this new form of communication, though."*

Persia swung her head to press her muzzle against Maya's. *"Yeah, me too. Shall we walk now?"*

Maya nodded and Persia grunted with what sounded like pleased satisfaction. She shifted on her powerful hindquarters and ambled off in a southeasterly direction. Maya followed, finally feeling like she belonged for the first time since she woke up in the wrong body.

Despite their size, they moved through the moonlit forest without causing much of a stir. Persia was better camouflaged in the moonlight with her mottled skin and stripes, but Maya damn near disappeared when she remained in the shadows. The nighttime critters must have been used to Persia's presence because the crickets kept singing and the small deer herd merely lifted their heads to watch them pass but went back to grazing on the grasses between the trees.

Maya was stiff from spending too much time in her human form and her body snapped and popped as muscles and ligaments stretched into their proper configurations.

Damn, I'm old. I gotta do this more often.

They made pretty good time down to the West Washakie River by following the stream that crossed in front of Persia's cabin. The night was cool enough to be comfortable, reminding Maya of the wintertime back in the Cretaceous. It never got terribly cold, but some of those winter nights had the temperatures of alpine summer nights. She breathed in the freshness of the air as she followed the female she'd grown to love.

Wait, love? Already?

Her human portion wanted to argue that it was too soon, but the dinosaur in her knew for certain Persia was her missing mate. The mate she'd dreamed of when just a young juvenile maiasaur migrating with her family into the warm, tropical southlands from the cooler north. She'd seen her mother nuzzling a male with a similar striped pattern to her own and understood the older female was choosing a mate. While the emotions weren't the same as she experienced in her human form, Maya understood there was attachment and connection between her mother and the male, and Maya wanted something like that for herself.

Before Maya could tell Persia what she'd discovered, they stepped out into a clearing that had been gridded off with wooden stakes and bright, neon flagging. Evidence of digging and bone removal showed in the perfectly square sides to the holes and the small piles of waste rock and dirt deposited outside the flagging. The moon made the site clearly visible, and the distinct shapes of at least three dinosaur skeletons lay in the hardpacked dirt.

"Oh my goodness. Are these your relatives, Persia?" Maya gazed down at the beautiful bones in the ground.

Persia nodded. *"They're my herdmates, my sisters."*

The word had a different nuance than simply siblings. Instead, it meant something more intimate, like the connection Maya had seen between her mother and the male. *She loved them.*

Sorrow damn near choked Maya and she rubbed her muzzle against Persia's shoulder. *"I'm so sorry, Persia."*

Persia took a deep breath and let it out in a long, humming exhale. *"Don't be. They are at peace, even if they were taken from me before I was ready. But I come out here a lot and talk to them, and I wanted you to meet them. I wanted them to see I've found someone special and I'm not alone anymore."*

"You're not?" Maya heard the surprise and hope in her own mind voice.

Persia pressed her forehead to Maya's, their breath mingling. *"Not anymore. I've found you and I feel the same connection with you that I had with them."* She stopped and drew back a little. *"Do you feel a connection?"*

The last question held a wealth of uncertainty and vulnerability, and Maya rumbled her own assent. *"Yes, I do. It's the first time I've felt this with anyone. I recognized it from watching my mother with her favorite male, but I never felt it until I met you. Then I knew right away."*

Persia rumbled a happy growl and pressed her muzzle against Maya's for a few moments before a mechanical sound intruded on their intimacy. Both their heads went up and Maya shifted to the side to look down the dirt road leading to the dig site. Vehicles approached, some large and some small, their lights cutting across the site. Persia bounded into the trees with Maya on her tale and they settled in to watch the intruders arrive.

Maya bumped Persia's side. *"Who the hell are these jokers?"*

Persia growled. *"I don't know, but I'll bet they have a connection to Krassobaki."*

Maya growled herself. *"If that's the case, I'm gonna shift and use my phone to take a video. I want evidence that jackass is trying to destroy our natural resources."*

Maya retreated behind a thicker clump of bushes and willed herself into her smaller, human body. It was a little like stuffing herself into a wetsuit and harder to do when Persia stood beside her in her full form. The world became a little more colorful, but the scents became muted to her nose.

A frisson of excitement went through her as Persia knelt to let her into the duffle bag to retrieve her phone as the vehicles pulled as close to the dig site as possible. Maya grabbed the cell and slipped behind one of the river boulders pushed up against the forest. Persia slunk into the trees, all but disappearing despite the headlights spearing the darkness.

Maya brought up the camera and took pictures of the vehicles, including their license plates and brand emblems. Then she hit record and got the faces of the men in the trucks.

"Woohoo! Grab the pickaxes and shovels, boys! We gonna dig us up some bones tonight."

One of the men threw back the last of a beer can and tossed it on the ground as he reached into the pickup bed for some sort of tool. The other men leapt to join him, half so damn tipsy they crashed to the ground and stumbled around like their legs had fallen asleep. Maya rolled her eyes, but kept the camera trained on them.

None of the vehicles had logos on their sides, but she'd seen a couple of them around town, and she recognized a few faces from the hardware store.

So, these are just good ole boys from Deadman. What the hell are they doing out here?

"Hey, Ty, hold up a bit. What are we supposed to do out here again?"

"Fuck, Chip, you're thick as a rock sometimes. Mr. Krassobaki paid us to fuck up those uppity university folks' dig sites. Said that would make them back off if their shit was gone and he'd get his permits to expand."

A deep growl came from the woods behind Maya, but the men couldn't hear it over their music and talking. That worked for Maya. She already had a recording of them with Krassobaki's name on it. But there wasn't time to waste on just recording the bastards. They were planning on destroying the burial site of Persia's sisters, and that wasn't gonna fly.

Maya waited long enough to get them moving on the site just so she had evidence of their intent to do damage. She ended the recording and stepped into the trees to shift back into her natural form.

"What are you doing, Maya?" Persia's voice came to her out of the darkness.

"I'm going to share the shit out of these boys."

"You can't. Then they'll know dinosaur shifters exist." Persia sounded uneasy though she kept her gaze focused on the men approaching the site.

"They're too drunk and none of them seem to have phones on them. They'd have to get back to their vehicles first. Let's have some fun. Growl."

The first guy raised a pickax above his head made Persia growl so menacingly that everyone shut up and paused.

"What the fuck was that?" Chip scanned the trees around the site, unable to pinpoint the sound.

There was a short period of silence as the men watched and listened, some swaying as the alcohol in their systems dismantled their balance.

"Aw, it ain't nothin'. Come on. Let's get this over with."

They moved closer and Persia growled again, this time louder and longer. Maya added her own growl, though it sounded more like a grinding whine than a growl.

I'm a freakin' herbivore, not a predator. I'm not supposed to sound scary.

"Oh shit, I heard that. What the fuck is it?" Another guy peered into the darkness. "Aldren, get in the truck and shine the spotlight into the trees, up there."

Maya suddenly had an idea and nudged Persia. *"Get out of the light. I'm gonna pull a Jurassic Park move."*

"What?" Persia tilted her head, a dinosaur equivalent of a raised eyebrow. *"What are you talking about?"*

"Just move back out of sight. You'll see what I'm talking about in a second."

Maya positioned herself with the trees framing one of her eyes, but keeping most of the rest of her body hidden. Then she waited. It didn't take long for the drunk boys to get the spotlight going and sure enough, they swung it right where Maya stood. The light hit her eye and her pupil shrank, leaving the rest of her brilliantly gold iris to glow.

"Oh shit. What the hell is that? Is that a goddamn eye?"

"Holy crap! It's a big fuckin' eye and it's way up in the fuckin' trees!"

"What the hell is that?"

Persia growled again and pushed against the trees, making them sway hard.

"Oh, fuck! It's a goddamn monster! I've seen this movie and I'm outta here!"

"Holy shit! It's 'Clever Girl!' Run!"

That was all it took. The men threw their tools into the backs of the trucks and clambered into the cabs. They cranked the engines and peeled out, damn near hitting each other in their desperation to get away. Dirt and rock flew as the vehicles churned up the roadway and disappeared into the darkness.

Maya chuckled as she rejoined Persia, rubbing her jaw along Persia's neck and shoulder. *"You were magnificent. Well done."*

"That was awesome! I'd forgotten about the Jurassic Park line." Persia rumbled a laugh as Maya shifted back into her human form to collect the phone and deposit it in the duffle bag.

"Easy, breezy, Clever Girl!" Maya snorted. "Damn right. Scared them right off."

Persia waited for her to shift again before she commented. *"We were damn lucky they hadn't brought guns with them, but I guess they figured fossils wouldn't fight back."* Persia nosed the bag. *"Did you get everything you need on the phone?"*

Maya nodded. "Yup. I'm gonna send it to all the city officials, some of the state officials, and the federal regulators in the USGS and BLM. Everyone's gonna know what Krassobaki has been up to." She zipped up the bag. "Let's go back to your place and celebrate with ice cream."

Persia shifted back to her human shape and grinned. "I have a better idea. How 'bout we go back to my place and celebrate with more than just ice cream."

Maya paused. "Oh, what did you have in mind?"

"It's date night, right?" Persia gather Maya in her arms. "I think some hot summer lovin' might be in order since we vanquished the vandals. Unless..." She stepped back, biting her lip.

"Unless what?" Maya lifted her chin.

"Unless you're not into... something like this... after, you know..."

"Pfft!" Maya threw the duffle bag onto the ground and wrapped her arms around Persia. "No way in hell am I gonna turn down a sexy, naked woman who's a total badass when defending what she loves." She leaned her forehead against Persia's. "Let's go back to your place and celebrate that greatness. Are you up for that?"

Persia's tension fled and she closed her eyes. "Yes, please, I'd love that."

CHAPTER FIVE

They shifted into their true forms and took their time ambling back through the forest to Persia's home. Maya loved the opportunity to just be herself in Persia's company, and enjoyed the patchwork of moonlight on Persia's striped scales as they headed back to her ranch house.

They shifted back at the porch and gathered up their clothes. Maya tried to swallow her disappointment at stuffing herself back into her human form, but the warmth of Persia's home took away most of it. She had to admit beds were better than leafy nests any day.

"Come in. Let me put the kettle on for some tea to warm us up."

Maya grinned as Persia headed for the kitchen without dressing. Worked for her. She loved a woman who didn't mind meandering around naked in her home.

"Rooibos, green, or black tea?"

"How 'bout..." Maya sauntered into the kitchen right up to Persia, swinging her hips in exaggerated steps. "I warm *you* up in other ways?"

Persia blinked as a smirk curled her lips and her nipples tightened. "Oh yeah? How are you going to do that?"

Maya reached up and ran her hand over Persia's hair held in the colorful hair bands. "Can I take these out?"

"Yes." Persia started with the first one. "But my hair will be all over the place."

"That works for me. I want to run my hands through it." Maya helped take out the rest of the bands until Persia's dark tresses fell around her face in waves. "Oh, that glorious. I love your long hair."

"I don't like it in my way, but without it, my head feels too light."

"I can see that." Maya gazed at her lover, taking in the loose blue and black hair as it cascaded over her shoulders to stop just above her breasts. "I like how it looks framing your face, though. Makes me want to kiss you."

"I'm not gonna stop you." Persia smirked, her russet brown eyes flashing with arousal.

Maya cupped Persia's face and brushed her lips across Persia's mouth. Instant awareness and connection flashed through her again, and she recognized both a kindred being and her fated mate. She deepened the kiss with a low moan, sliding her tongue across Persia's in a desperate caress, needing more.

Persia pulled back and her eyes glowed almost crimson. "Maya, I need you. I need you in my bed right now."

Maya's nipples tightened to hard tips as arousal shot through her. "I'm yours."

A quick flash of a grin, and Persia dragged her down the short hallway to her bedroom. Maya expected something no-frills, earthy colors, and minimalist given what she knew of Persia. But the room they entered looked like a tropical paradise.

Large potted palms graced the corners of the room, giving the impression of dense jungle foliage. A humidifier pumped out warm steam from the corner behind a bureau, while a reading chair hid between a potted fern and a small table. The walls had been covered with tropical foliage wallpaper and the bedspread matched along with the chair. It smelled like home to Maya and she gave a sigh of comfort.

"Wow, this room is great. How do you ever go out? I swear, if this was my room, I'd never leave." Maya didn't release Persia's hand, but she turned to look at everything as Persia switched on the recessed lighting. "Oh my glory! It's like a night garden."

Persia closed the door behind her and gathered Maya into her arms, pressing her breasts against Maya's back. "It was just a place to sleep away from the dry human world. But now with you here, it's truly a sanctuary."

Maya grinned. "Oh yeah? I like the sound of that." She pulled Persia into her arms. "I want to enjoy it with you." She thumbed Persia's nipples. "Starting with these."

She dipped her head and sucked one pink peak into her mouth, laving it with her tongue. Persia moaned as she grasped Maya's hips to hold on, thrusting her chest deeper into Maya's mouth. The scents of sun-warmed stone and water lilies intensified as Persia's arousal increased, and Maya reveled in them.

"Oh glory, Maya. I want you so much."

Maya let the nipple pop from her mouth as she pulled back. "Oh yeah? It's a good thing, because I want you. Let's move to the bed so you don't fall down, because I'm not nearly done with you and I want to take my time."

She expected Persia to bound onto the bed, but the woman sauntered, swinging her hips with the few steps it took. Maya's mouth watered with her sexy moves, and she followed like a dog on a leash.

Or a hadrosaur after tender waterlilies.

Persia pulled back the covers and climbed onto the bed. She spread her arms and her legs, and her pretty pink pussy glistened in the tropical lighting. The water lily fragrance hit Maya's limited nose and she damn near swooned. She crawled onto the bed and settled between Persia's legs with a saucy grin.

"Thank you for a such a lovely display and buffet." She kissed Persia's inner thighs. "I love this treat. Are you ready for me to feast?"

"Oh, glory, yes." Persia sat up and grasped Maya's head. "But I need a kiss first."

"Oh, I'm gonna kiss you. You can be sure of that."

Persia chuckled. "Yeah, but I want one on my mouth first."

Maya pushed up enough to meet Persia's lips and fell into her kiss from the moment they touched. It was soft and sweet, yet heady and arousing as their tongues tangled in the ancient dance of love. The scent of waterlilies filled Maya's nose as Persia's unique flavor filled her mouth, spiking her own arousal.

When they broke apart to catch their breath, Maya smirked. "Okay, now I really want to taste your pussy.

I've been smelling your arousal and I just can't wait any longer."

She dropped until her face was in line with Persia's mound and didn't wait. She leaned forward and sucked Persia's clit into her mouth, rubbing it with her tongue.

"Oh my glory!" Persia let herself flop into the pillows and her whole body shivered.

Maya took that as a sign to continue so she released Persia's clit and laved her sensitive folds with the tip of her tongue. Persia whined and shivered, and Maya reveled in the sweet flavor of Persia's cream. Her pussy was such a delicate pink, and the waterlily flavor intensified at her slit. Maya couldn't get enough of it, but she wanted to savor and take her time. Her own pussy clenched with desperate arousal, but Maya forced her attention on her lover's vulva.

She stroked her tongue between the labia before returning to Persia's clit to apply pressure. Persia rocked her hips gently, trying to get more friction, but Maya backed off and used the flat of her tongue to keep up the teasing caresses.

Persia's whine became almost petulant as Maya tickled the entrance to Persia's vagina with teasing touches. Persia rocked her hips with insistence, and Maya inwardly laughed.

I know what you want, my lovely beauty.

She slid one hand up to stroke Persia's vulva while she sucked on Persia's clit. She peeled the labia apart and let her fingers caress the soft flesh. Persia whimpered and rocked her hips in time with Maya's fingers. Maya licked the labia and her own fingers before she slid them into Persia's grasping pussy, and Persia wailed.

Maya curled her fingers to find Persia's G-spot as she sucked on Persia's clit. She stroked her fingers in and out of Persia's pussy slowly, building up the sensation along with suckling her clit. Persia rocked her hips in time with Maya's strokes, whimpering her needy call.

Maya sucked harder on Persia's clit and increased the frequency of her strokes as Persia tightened her hands in the bedcovers.

Oh, she's close.

Maya curled her fingers again and stroked harder against Persia's G-spot, and Persia's pussy clamped down on her hand. She threw back her head and screamed as her hips rocked harder against Maya's face. Maya drank down the flood of cream from Persia's pussy and rode out the hard orgasm tightening Persia's body.

At last her lover relaxed, her legs flopping to the bed in exhausted euphoria. Maya licked up all Persia's excess cream off her fingers and sat back. She loved the satisfied look on Persia's face and the heavily lidded russet eyes.

"You're so beautiful when you're satisfied." Maya crawled up the bed to gather Persia into her arms.

"Partially satisfied." The words didn't match the look on Persia's face.

"Partially satisfied? What the hell does that mean?" Unease settled in Maya's gut.

A slow smirk curled Persia's lips. "It means that I need to make sure you're just as satisfied as I am and I can't do that until I've enjoyed that pussy of yours, too."

Relief poured through Maya, loosening her body. "Hey, I'm not adverse to that at all."

"Good." Persia rolled over and kissed Maya soundly. "Because now it's my turn."

CHAPTER SIX

Persia watched Maya's expression. It changed from uncertainty, to relief, to intense arousal, and excitement flashed through Persia at the power she had over her beautiful lover. Maya's olive skin glowed in the tropical lighting, and Persia had never been so glad for all the money and effort she'd used in making her bedroom a sanctuary. It felt even more so with Maya in it.

Persia took a moment to take in Maya's human form. Her full breasts had dusky brown nipples that reminded Persia of juicy berries meant to be savored. The thick tresses of deep brown hair spread across her green sheets and made her mouth water.

"You're so beautiful. I can't even put it into words."

She ran her hands over Maya's chest, playing with the dusky nipples and enjoying how the full breasts jiggled with each breath. She loved the way the light and shadows played along Maya's curves, and Persia leaned forward to trail kisses over the soft mounds. The scent of Maya's skin—forest pines and sun-touched moss—filled Persia's nose and she nuzzled the silken skin between Maya's breasts, inhaling deeply.

Maya's arms wrapped around Persia's shoulders as Persia took a hard nipple into her mouth. She suckled gently, pulling at the tip with her teeth. Maya rumbled what could only be called a musical purr and arched her back. Persia took advantage and massaged the other breast with her free hand.

"Oh, yes, Persia. Just like that."

Persia switched to the other breast with her mouth and massaged the first one with her other hand as the scent of sun-touched moss deepened. Persia trailed her other hand down Maya's belly and slid her fingers over Maya's mound to dip between her legs. She found a warm, wet paradise, and stroked it, making them both moan.

"You're so wet for me, Maya." Persia pulled her hand up to her mouth and licked Maya's cream off her fingers. "Oh my glory, you taste divine."

"Just like you." Maya panted, her breasts jiggling more. Persia's pussy clenched with her renewed arousal.

"I need to feast on you. And at risk at repeating what you did to me, I'm going to eat your pussy with abandon and make you come all over my face."

"Hey, when something works well, who am I to complain?" Maya grinned.

"Excellent response." Persia slid down Maya's body and inhaled deeply at the juncture of her thighs. "Perfection."

Maya laughed but it turned into a moan when Persia sealed her mouth over Maya's vulva. Persia feasted, licking and suckling on Maya's clit and labia. Maya's moans turned to cries as she licked between the labia and she rocked her hips against Persia's face. The scent of sun-touched moss filled the air around Persia's face and she breathed it in as she peeled Maya's labia apart with her thumbs.

Then she slid her tongue deep into Maya's sheath.

She must have worked Maya up to a fever pitch because only a few thrusts of Persia's tongue and Maya flooded her mouth with a torrent of cream. Persia drank it down and made a vow to make Maya come as often as she could because her cream was like ambrosia. Persia savored Maya's earthy flavor and licked Maya's labia clean.

Persia wiped her mouth and moved up to gather Maya into her arms, feeling a deep sense of satisfaction and contentment. She'd rarely found someone who could please her sexually, and give her a great sense of satisfaction in serving them. Most of her sexual encounters had been quickies, something meant to take the edge off so she could continue on her way.

But with Maya, who gave great orgasms, it was more like she'd found the perfect sexual partner, and a partner who Persia wanted more time with. A woman who knew her quirks and didn't make it weird.

Persia sighed happily. "Perfection."

Maya chuckled. "What is?"

"You."

"Me?" Maya raised her eyebrows. "How am I perfection?"

"Well..." Persia started counting on her fingers. "You're gorgeous. You're smart. You're funny. You're crafty. You taste fucking delicious, and you give great orgasms. See? Perfection."

"Well, when you put it like that..." Maya grinned as she rolled onto her side. "I think the same about you, Persia. I really enjoyed tonight."

Persia smirked. "Even when we had to scare the shit out of those good ole boys?"

"Especially then." Maya's smile softened and she trailed her fingers over Persia's arm. "But mostly being with you. We could be sitting outside drinking tea or chasing hoodlums off of paleontological sites. As long as I'm with you, it's the perfect day."

Warmth filled Persia's chest and she rolled over to brush her lips across Maya's. "Yeah, that sounds like a perfect day to me, too."

"I love you, Persia."

Surprise slapped Persia between the eyes as she stared at Maya.

"You do?"

Maya nodded. "I do. Very much."

After the initial jolt of uncertainty, Persia found herself comfortable with the idea of loving Maya and spending a lot of time with her. More midnight strolls in their true forms. More snuggling in bed. More standing together to defend the land and town they loved.

"Good. Because I love you, too, and I want to spend a lot more time with you chasing hoodlums, running the bed and breakfast, and having sex. Not necessarily in that order."

Maya grinned. "Can we have more sex? Like right now?"

"Oooh, you want more already?" Persia leaned over and kissed Maya deeply. "I think that can be arranged. I aim to give you as many orgasms as I can tonight."

"Bring it on."

And Persia did.

CHAPTER SEVEN

Persia grinned as she read The Deadman Daily. She normally only got the online paper, but the head-lines were too delicious to not buy the hardcopy.

We Are Not for Sale: Small Town in Wyoming Tells Big Billionaire to Scrap Retreat Plans

DEADMAN, WY. Billionaire Clifford Krassobaki has had a bad week. Not only were his plans and permits for expansion of his palatial resort denied, but he was caught paying local thugs to destroy local paleontological and archaeological sites in an effort to demoralize his detractors.

Krassobaki's thugs were caught on video attempting to destroy a site watched over by the Friends of Deadman Paleontology director, Persia Walker. Walker and a friend were visiting the site when men in vehicles arrived and attempted to destroy the bones in the ground.

"We take our paleontology very seriously," Walker said. "Once they admitted they'd been paid by Krassobaki to destroy the site in an effort to force his permits through, we had grounds to throw the book at him."

Krassobaki was charged with destruction of a federally protected site under the Paleontological Resources Preservation Act (PRPA). In addition to hefty fines, Krassobaki was indicted for tax evasion, money laundering, and his palatial estate was hounded by protestors. He's been forced to put the lands on the market as he faces indictment. No word if there are any buyers willing to face an irate town.

In a joint statement given to police, the lead perpetrators of the destruction, Ty Lindhurst of Afton, WY, and Chip Huffman of Deadman, WY, claim there were monsters straight out of *Jurassic Park* in the woods that night.

Breathalyzer tests showed all the men with blood alcohol levels of 0.09, well above the legal

```
limit to be operating heavy ma-
chinery. Police investigated but
found no evidence of 'monsters'
in the woods. All the men were
arrested with DWIs and fined
$10,000 under PRPA. No bail was
set."
```

"Now, that is a beautiful sight." Maya leaned against Persia's shoulder to read the paper. "We need to keep a copy of that in a scrap book somewhere."

"Oh, hell yeah." Persia tilted her head. "I suppose we could frame it."

"Nah, I don't want to display it. It wouldn't go with the décor in the B&B. But I definitely want a copy so I can look back on it and smile." Maya grinned as she headed back into her kitchen. "Can I get you some peppermint tea before we talk to the kids?"

Persia took a deep breath as she followed. "Yeah, I'd love some tea. But are you sure you want to tell them?"

"Absolutely. Are you afraid they're going to freak out?" Maya put the kettle on to boil before she pulled out the loose-leaf peppermint tea she'd bought specifically for Persia.

Persia bit her lip as she settled in the chair at the table. "Yeah, kinda. I mean, it's kinda a big deal—especially in Wyoming. You don't think they'll freak out?"

Maya smiled warmly. "No, I know them pretty well. I think they'll totally take it in stride. Even if they're adopted and not in the same boat, I think they'll be delighted." She laid a hand on Persia's arm. "Are you nervous?"

Persia nodded. "A littl ' When Maya raised an eyebrow, she amended, "Okay, a lot. But it probably seems really sudden to them. We've only known each other for a few weeks."

"They'll be fine with it. You'll see. They won't freak out."

Persia wasn't so sure. What they had to tell the mammalian kids could blow their minds and she didn't want to have to let Maya go. Or get her in trouble.

I just found her. I can't lose her, and I don't want her kids to hate her. Or me.

All the satisfaction of knowing Krassobaki was done in Deadman, Wyoming, drained away at the thought of how Maya's kids would take their news. She'd never had to expose herself to humans before, and knowing what humans tended to do to beings beyond their understanding, dread filled her belly and she swallowed hard against rising bile.

"When will they be home?"

Maya opened her mouth to reply when a door opened and footsteps sounded in the hall.

"Hey, Mom, we're home. Are you here?"

Maya grinned. "Yeah, we're in the kitchen. Come on back."

Quinn and Bailey appeared, hung their book bags on the hooks near the backdoor and immediately came to Maya for hugs. She held each one for longer than most humans tolerated, and Persia hoped she'd eventually get hugs, too.

If they still want me around after we tell them our news.

"So, how were your days? Good?" Maya kissed both kids on the foreheads before getting back to her cooking.

Both teens launched into a rundown of their days with enthusiasm as Maya finished preparing a vegetable frittata for supper. They were eating early so they could go to the Art in the Park craft show that night. Persia fidgeted as the kids shared the events of their day, but as they wound down, her restlessness increased. Maya drew a deep breath to keep her own energy calm.

"So, what did you want to talk to us about?" Quinn popped a grape into her mouth from the bowl in the middle of the table.

"Well…" Maya came to stand beside Persia, resting a hand on her shoulder. "We wanted to let you know that, uh…" She shot a look at Persia before she gathered her courage. "That we're dating now."

"That's great!" Bailey grinned. "It's about damn time. Persia is over here all the time. I figured it was something like that."

Persia let her breath out. "Oh, good. I was worried y'all would be uneasy about it."

Quinn snorted. "Uneasy? Why? It's obvious you both like each other a lot, and I haven't seen Mom this happy, ever. I think it's awesome." She glanced at her brother and he nodded. "Did you think we'd have a problem that you're lesbians?"

Maya nodded. "It was a concern. You know how people get when they learn folks don't fit their world view. Something flips in their brains, and they lose all sense. We didn't want you to be uncomfortable with our relationship."

Bailey grimaced. "Yeah, people are stupid. I see it all the time on the internet. Apparently, there are humans out there who think if you delete something from the internet, it's gone forever." He rolled his eyes and shook his head.

"But this is great. To be honest, I thought you were going to tell us you were dinosaur shifters. But this is totally cool, too."

Maya raised her eyebrows while Persia gaped. "What?" They shared a look. "Why would you say that?"

Quinn shrugged. "Because of the *Jurassic Park* reference the drunks said in the paper today, and because I've seen you shift into a big ass Maiasaur, Mom. Love the stripes, by the way."

Maya's jaw dropped. "You've seen me *shift*? When...? How...? Why didn't you say anything?"

Quinn and Bailey exchanged a look. "Because it was a totally natural thing that you do. I mean, we smelled that you were some kind of shifter, but we didn't know which kind."

Persia blinked. "There are different kinds of shifters?"

"Uh, yeah." Bailey pushed his glasses up his nose and gave them a perplexed smile. "I thought that's why you adopted us. Because you knew we weren't human." He paused. "You knew we weren't human, right?"

Maya sank into the chair beside Persia. "What?"

"Oh my glory, Mom didn't know!" Bailey shot a look at his sister. "I told you."

"You really didn't know, Mom?" Quinn had a goofy smile on her face.

Maya shook her head as she took Persia's hand. "I had no idea. You just felt right when I found you and I couldn't leave you on the streets." Maya reached for Quinn's hand. "I'm so sorry I didn't realize. Are you a dinosaur like we are?"

Quinn shook her head. "Nope. We're bears."

"Bears..." Maya gazed at her kids.

"Yup, big, fuzzy Grizzly bears." Quinn nodded. "Okay, so we're not as big as you when you shift, but yeah. I'm darker brown than Bailey, who trends toward golden brown like Irish coffee. Which is where he got his name."

Bailey shot a look at Persia. "What kind of dinosaur are you?"

Persia gave him a bemused smirk. "Parasaurolophus."

"Cool! That's the one with the huge crest that makes musical sounds, right?"

"Uh, yeah, that's right." Persia nodded.

"Way cool. Hey, Mom. When's the frittata gonna be done? I want to take a shower before we go to Art in the Park." Bailey got up and grabbed a chilled bottle of water from the fridge.

"Uh, soon. Fifteen minutes, max." Maya got up and checked on the food.

"Great. I'll take a quick shower." He waved as he headed out of the room.

"Well, that went better than I thought it would." Persia shook her head. "Bear shifters. At least I got it right that you were mammals."

"Yup." Quinn beamed. "So, are we all going to run the Fossil Beds B&B together, as one big happy shifter family?" Quinn beamed.

"I guess we are." Maya grinned. "Just remember in this paleo household: there are so many beds, but so little time."

She laughed as everyone groaned at her Mom joke.

The End

AUTHOR'S NOTE

W hile my town of Deadman, Wyoming is fictional, earlier this year, in Bondurant, Wyoming, an actual billionaire name Joe Ricketts tried to expand on his property to make a resort (adding a restaurant, gymnasium, bunkhouse, and cabin village). The county commissioner Doug Vickrey put a stop to Ricketts' delusions of grandeur by telling him, "Remember, some things are not for sale. Folks, I'm going to tell you right now, I am one of those things. I am not for sale. So, I would like Mr. Ricketts to know that with all his wealth there are some things in this world money cannot buy, and by God I'm one of them."

It was a beautiful thing and gave me the inspiration to write this tale. I hope you enjoy Maya and Persia's story, and know that yeah, we Wyomingites do stand up to big money every now and again. Happy reading!

About Siobhan Muir

Siobhan Muir lives in Cheyenne, Wyoming, with her husband, two daughters, a kitten who thinks he's a dog, a cat who's not impressed with him, and the dog who just wants to go for a walk. In previous lives, Siobhan has been an actor at the Colorado Renaissance Festival, a field geologist in the Aleutian Islands, and restored inter-planetary imagery at the USGS. She's hiked to the top of Mount St. Helens and to the bottom of Meteor Crater. Siobhan writes kick-ass adventure with hot sex for men and women to enjoy. She believes in happily ever after, redemption, and communication, all of which you will find in her paranormal romance and dauntless romance stories.

Connect with Siobhan online at:
https://siobhanmuir.com/
Facebook
Instagram
Siobhan's Blog

Bluesky

Mastodon

MeWe

Patreon

Or sign up for her newsletter to get excerpts and cover reveals and other fun extras.

NEWSLETTER

OTHER BOOKS BY SIOBHAN MUIR

Other Books by Siobhan Muir

Her Devoted Vampire

The Sorceress of Song and Flame

Mr. Fixit's Billionaire

Fossil Beds Bed & Breakfast

The Dreadstone King

Bad Boys of Beta Squad Series

Bronco's Rough Ride

The Navy's Ghost

Rimshot's Hard Target

Bam-Bam's Inked Hart

Deli's Take Out

Callowwood Pack Series

Queen Bitch of the Callowwood Pack

The Callowwood Canine Caper

Cloudburst Colorado Series

A Hell Hound's Fire

The Beltane Witch

Christmas I.C.E. Magic

Cloudburst Ice Magic

Cloudburst Coffee & Spa

Courting the Dragon Widow

The Samhain Soldier

Concrete Angels MC Series

My Forever Cocky Biker Encounter

Dude With a Cool Car

Angel Ink

The Concrete Angel

Running From the Texas Millionaire

Elemental Hearts Series

Wildfire's Heart

A Timeless Heart

Rifts Series
Take the Reins
A Centaur's Solstice Wish
In Death's Shadow

Silver State Mysteries Series
Second Chance Succubus

Summit Springs Sapphic Romance
Broken Chains
In Plain Sight

Triple Star Ranch Series
Rope a Falling Star
Star Light, Star Bright
Star Spangled Banner

Ultimate Recon Series
Darwin's Evolution

Warbler Peninsula Series
Order of the Dragon
The Valkyrie's Sword
Burning Yuletide

The Ivory Road Serial

A Walk in the Sand

Outback Dreams

A Dance Between Worlds

The Karobis Calls

Coming Soon

The Siren Queen (Sirens, Inc. #1)

The Siren and the Scientist (Sirens, Inc. #2)

www.ingramcontent.com/pod-product-compliance
Lightning Source LLC
Chambersburg PA
CBHW022040170626
46808CB00003B/1293